SO-AZO-446

MYSTERY at the ZOO

Written by Robyn Supraner
Illustrated by Bert Dodson

Troll Associates

Copyright © 1979 by Troll Associates
All rights reserved. No part of this book may be used or reproduced
in any manner whatsoever without written permission from the publisher.
Printed in the United States of America.

Troll Associates, Mahwah, N.J.

Library of Congress Catalog Card Number: 78-60126

MYSTERY at the ZOO

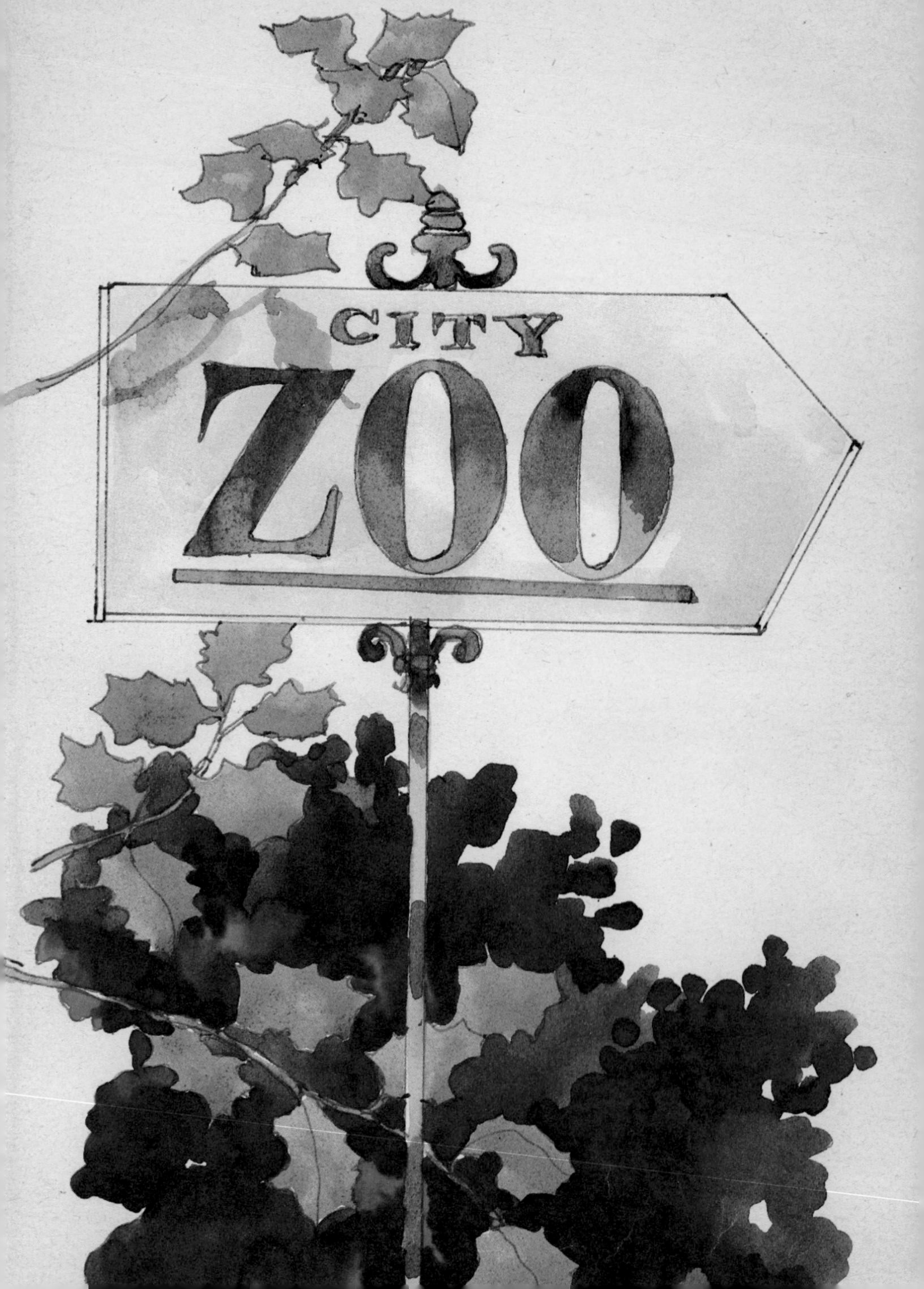
CITY
ZOO

Every day when school was out, Michael Andrew Kevin McCuller would head straight for the zoo.

He would hurry past the zebras and the giraffes and the monkeys.

He would skip past the elephants and the bears and the rhinoceros.

He would wave to the balloon man and the woman who sold peanuts and popcorn.

He would run through a tunnel and over a bridge. He wouldn't stop running until he reached the lion's cage.

Then Michael Andrew Kevin McCuller would put down his books and say, "Good afternoon, Simba. Tell me, how are you feeling today?"

And Simba would slowly rise to his feet, toss his tawny mane, blink his golden eyes, and answer:

"I am very well, thank you, Michael. But I do miss Africa."

Then Michael Andrew Kevin McCuller would sit on the rail near Simba's cage and listen to stories of far-off Africa, until the sun set and it was time to go home.

Simba told him of the bush country where he was born, and of the grassland where he grew up.

He told him how the rain smelled, and how the hyena howled.

He spoke of his family and his friends.

But most of all, he talked about Serena. "Ah, Michael!" he would say. "She was sleek and graceful and strong. She was beautiful. If only I could see her again."

Then one day, when Michael arrived at the zoo, he saw a big crowd around Simba's cage.

The zookeeper was blowing his whistle.

People were shouting. Children were crying. Everyone was talking at once.

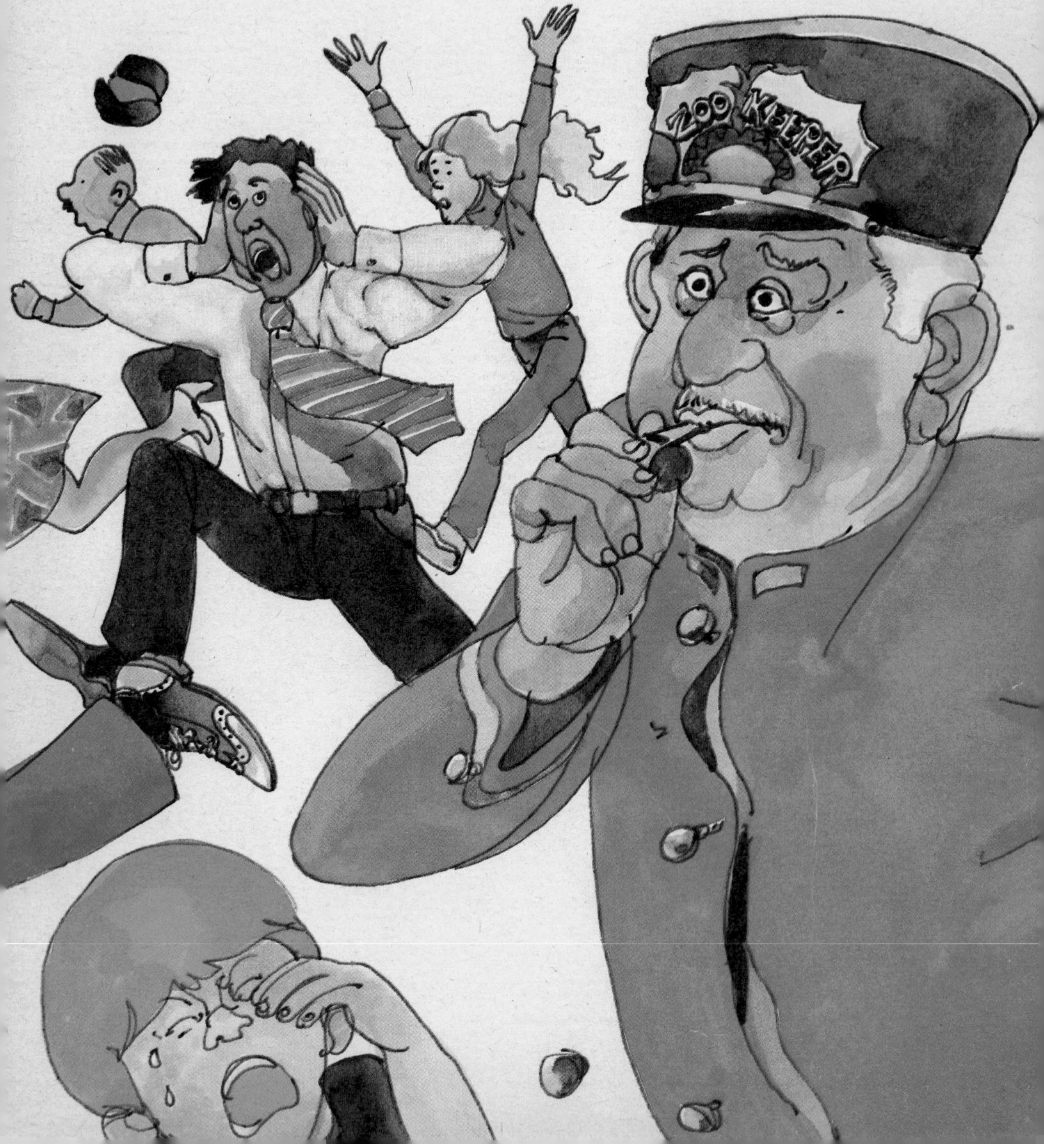
ZOO KEEPER

"What happened? What is the matter?"
Michael called to a woman who was running
with a baby in her arms.

"Haven't you heard?" the woman
shouted back. "The lion has escaped! Run
for your life if you know what is good for
you!"

Men in blue uniforms arrived in a truck.
They carried guns and nets. They spoke to
the zookeeper. They looked very serious.

Michael tried to hear what they were
saying, but he was too far away.

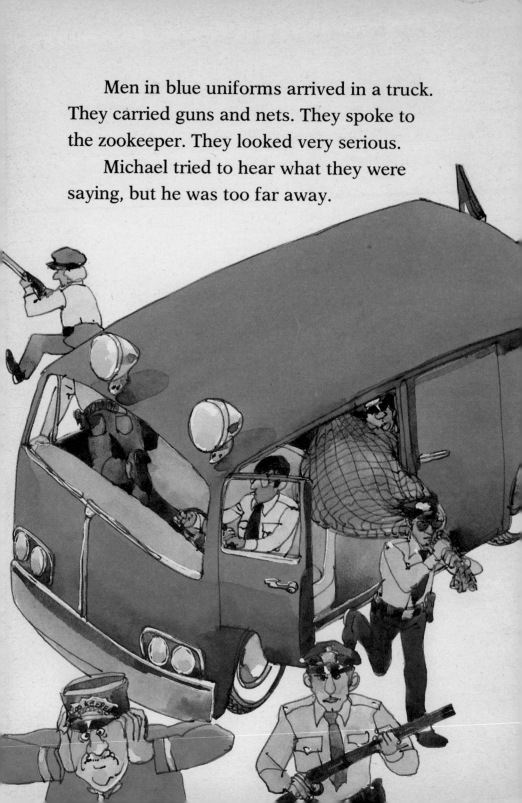

A man standing next to him leaned down and said, "Don't worry, kid. Nobody will hurt Simba. Unless he has to."

Suddenly, Michael was frightened. Simba was in danger!

"Not one of us is safe until that lion is behind bars!" said a woman in a yellow polka-dotted dress.

"We must stay in our houses and lock our doors!" cried a woman who was trying to hold three balloons, and two wiggly children.

"We should offer a reward for his capture!" called a woman, who was wearing a large hat with feathers.

"Yes! Yes!" cried the others.

"One hundred dollars!" someone shouted.

"Two hundred and fifty!" shouted another.

"Five hundred!" shouted the woman with the feathers in her hat. "Five hundred dollars for the lion. Dead or alive!"

It was then, at that very minute, that Michael knew he had to find Simba. He had to find him before anyone else did, or there was no telling what might happen.

Michael left the zoo. He had to think. He had to remember everything Simba had told him. Somewhere, in those stories of Africa, was the clue to where Simba was hiding.

Michael thought and thought. He thought of the bush country. He thought of the plains.

"Aha!" said Michael. "I know just where to find him."

He ran down the street until he came to a big stone building. The sign said:

THE ZOO SOCIETY
Lecture Today:
"THE AFRICAN PLAINS"
Everyone Welcome

Michael went inside. He walked into a large room with many people. He looked around, but he did not see Simba.

He spoke to a man who was wearing a brightly colored dashiki.

"Please, sir," said Michael. "I am looking for a lion. He has escaped from the zoo, and I am worried about him."

"I am sorry, little brother," said the man in the dashiki. "I have not seen your lion. But I will ask the others."

The man spoke into a microphone. "Ladies and gentlemen," he said. "Your attention, please. I have just found out that a lion has escaped from the zoo . . ."

Before he could say another word,
everyone jumped up. People screamed and
shouted and pushed and shoved. They
climbed on top of each other. They ran in
every direction.

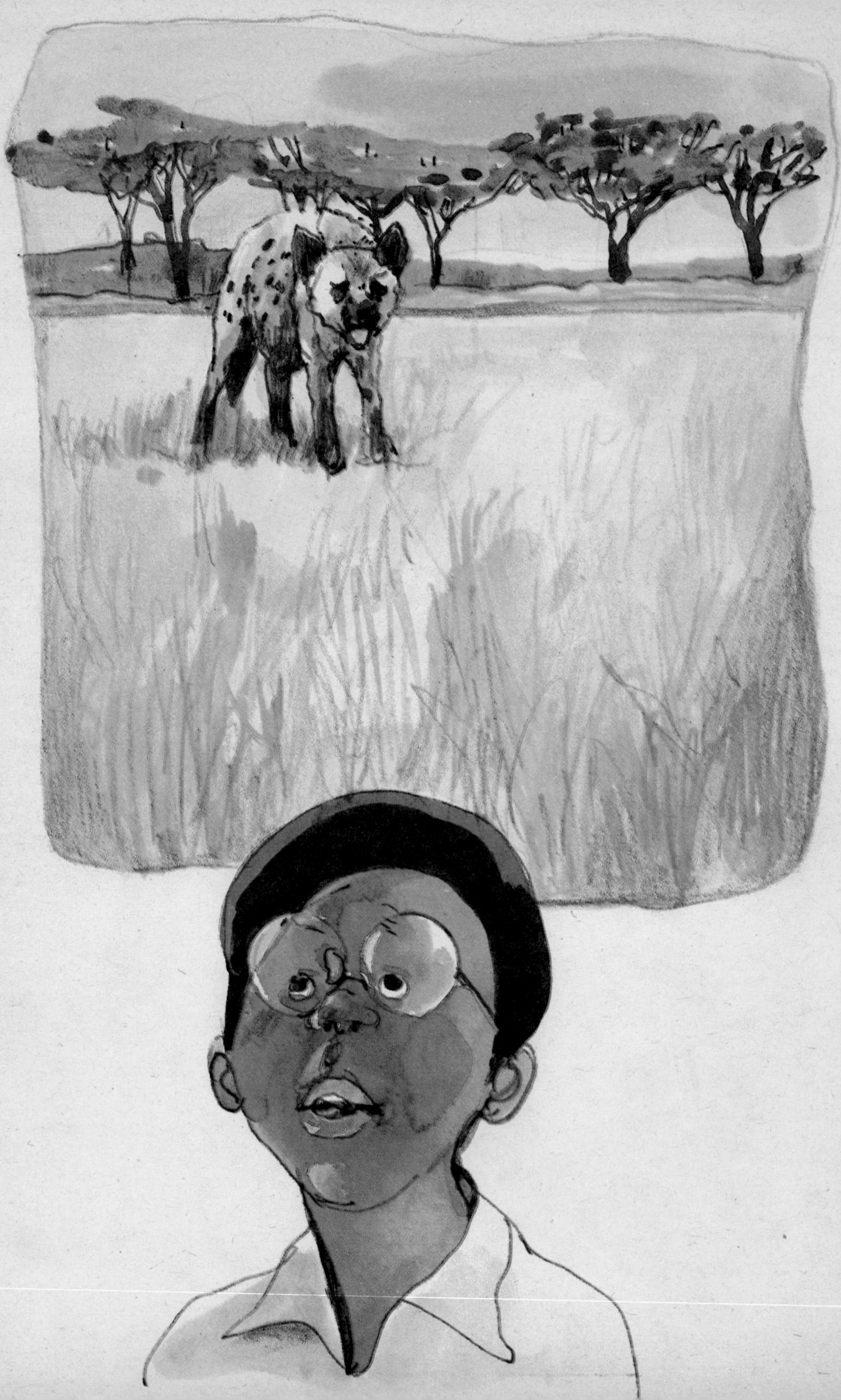

Soon the room was empty.

Michael said he was sorry to have caused so much trouble. The man in the dashiki said he was sorry, too. They shook hands. Then Michael said goodbye.

Michael thought and thought. He thought of how the rain smelled in Africa. He thought of how the dry grass rustled in the wind. He thought of how the hyena howled.

"Aha!" said Michael. "I know just the place to find Simba."

He crossed three streets. He turned two corners. He ran and ran, until he came to a big gray building. A sign said:

THE MUSEUM OF
NATURAL HISTORY

Michael went inside. He walked through the hall of dinosaurs. He saw a woolly mammoth. He saw a saber-toothed tiger. But he did not see Simba.

He went into one room, down a hall, and then out another room.

He saw all kinds of things.

He saw a polar bear, a walrus, and a penguin.

At last, he came to a large room. A sign
in the doorway said:

   THE AFRICAN VELDT.

Michael crossed his fingers, and went in.

It was just as Simba had said.

Antelopes and elephants were gathered round a water hole.

There were zebras and giraffes.

There were cheetahs and jackals and ring-tailed wildcats—and the largest cat of all, the African lion.

Michael closed his eyes. He heard a
hyena howl. He heard a lion roar. He
smelled the rain. A shiver ran up his back.

When he opened his eyes, it was quiet.
Nothing moved. The veldt was as still as a
painting, and Simba was nowhere in sight.

Michael stopped a woman. "Have you seen a lion?" he asked her.

The woman pointed to the glass case.

"Not that lion," said Michael. "I mean a real lion."

"Try the zoo," said the woman, and
hurried on her way.

Michael left the museum. He walked and walked. He did not look where he was going. He did not see the sign until he bumped into it.

COME TO THE CIRCUS

see

ACROBATS & CLOWNS

LIONS & TIGERS

Michael bought a ticket. He went inside
and sat down.

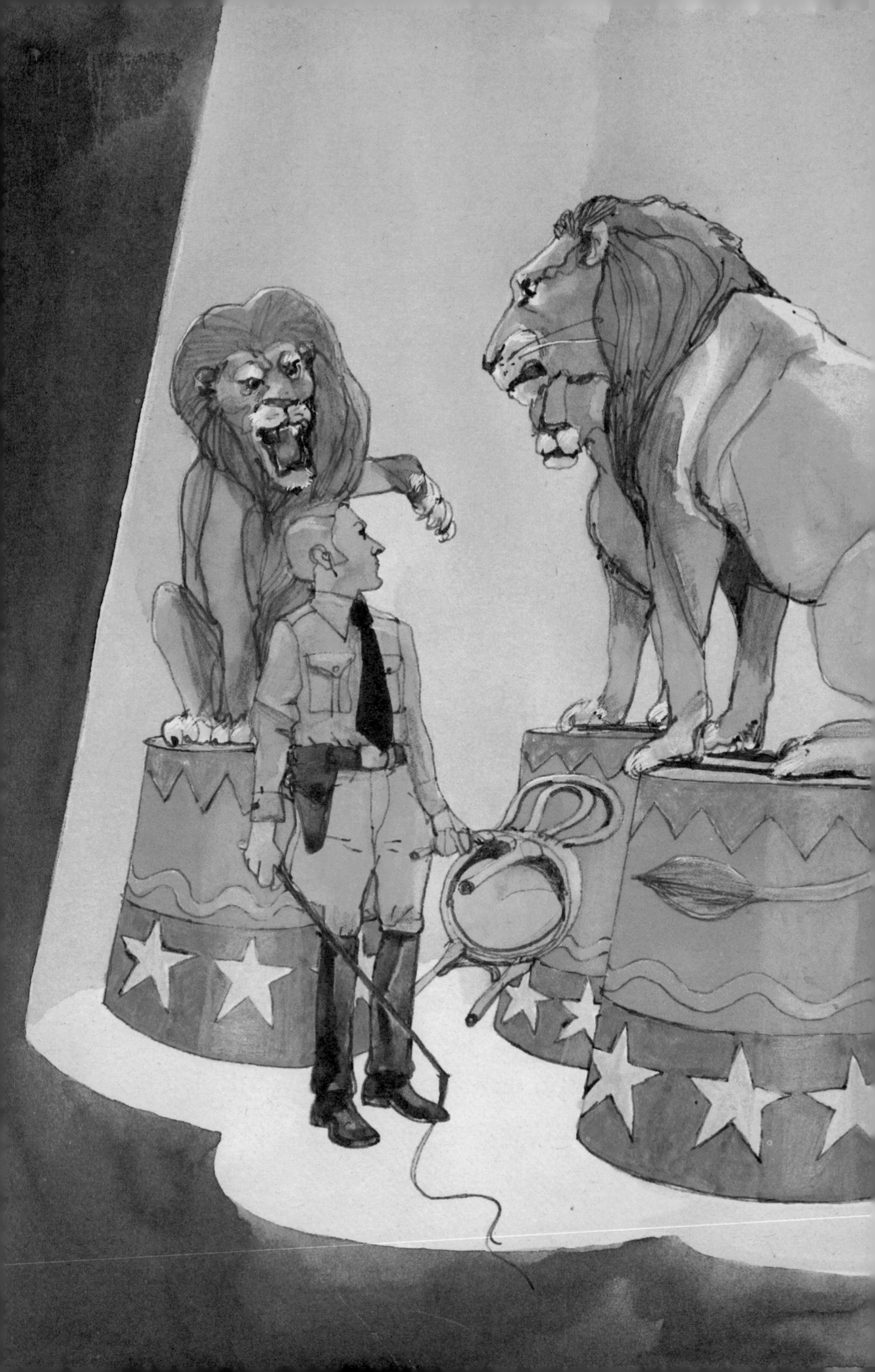

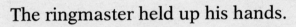

The ringmaster held up his hands.

"Ladies and gentlemen!" he said. "From the wilds of Africa, we bring to you the one and only Buddy Brave and his ferocious African lions!"

The lion tamer cracked his whip. The lions tossed their tawny manes. They blinked their golden eyes. They leaped to their stools, and spread their sharp claws.

Michael looked for Simba. He was not there.

Then a drum rolled. A trumpet blared—
and a lovely lioness stepped into the center
ring. She was sleek and graceful and strong.
She was beautiful.

A hush fell over the audience. For a
moment, nobody moved.

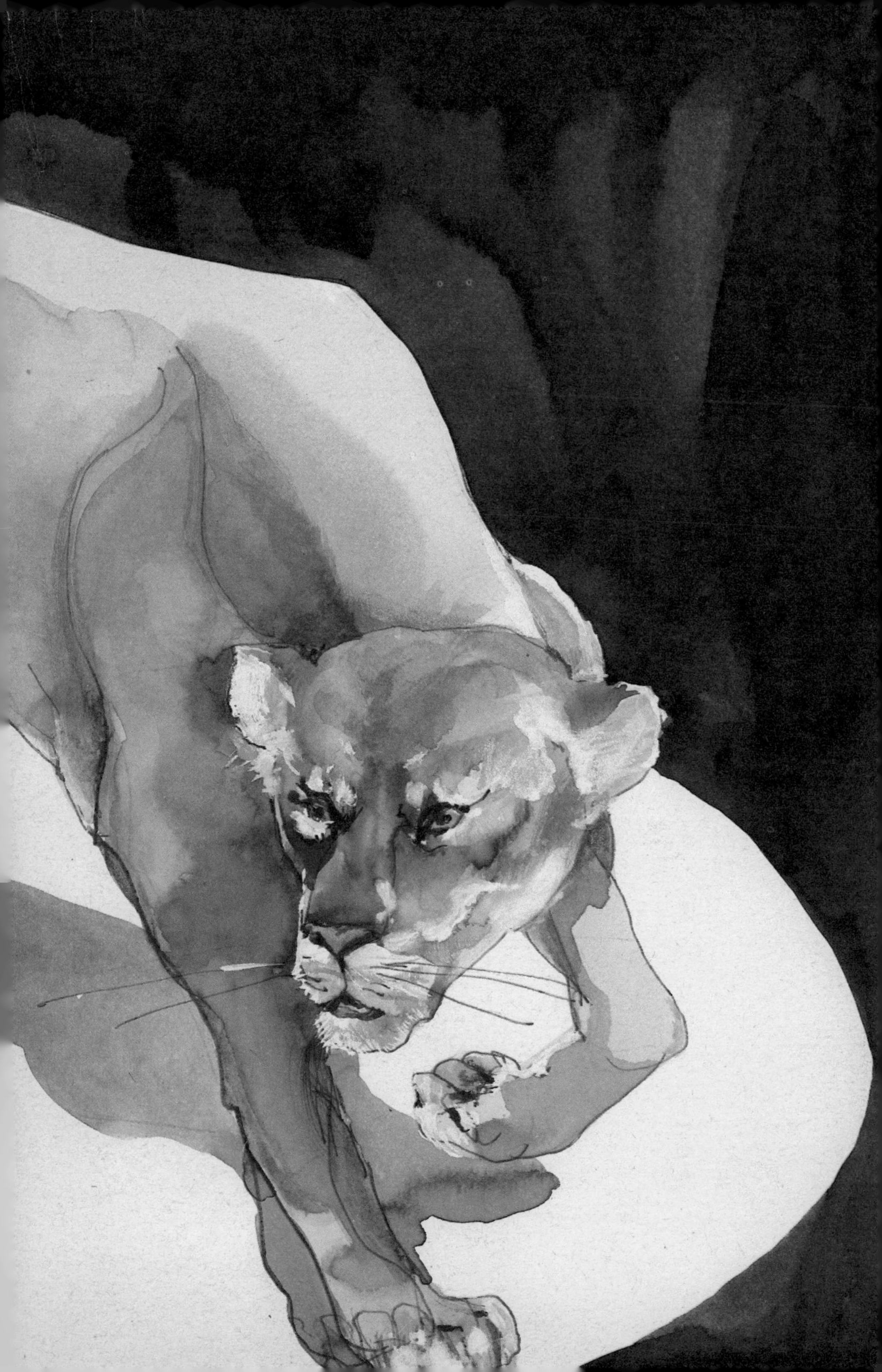

R

Then a sound came from the top row of the grandstand. It sounded like the roaring of a train. It sounded like the rumbling of an earthquake. It shook the circus tent.

Michael looked up, up, up. High above the crowd sat Simba. His golden eyes blazed

like a flame. He had come to see the beautiful lioness. He had come to see Serena.

People were frightened when they saw the mighty lion. They ran away as fast as they could.

Animal trainers ran in with a heavy net. They threw the net over Simba's head.

"Stop!" cried Michael, when he saw what was happening. "Stop! Oh, please stop!"

The guards did not hear him. They drew the net tighter, and led Simba away.

Michael sat down on a bench. He covered his face with his hands, and cried.

Soon he felt a hand on his shoulder. He looked up. It was Buddy Brave, the lion tamer.

Michael told him all about Simba and Serena. He told him of the many times he had heard Simba say, "Ah, Michael! She was beautiful. If only I could see her again."

"I have an idea," the lion tamer said. He
bent down and whispered into Michael's ear.
"Yes!" said Michael. "Oh, yes!"

The next day, there was a lot of excitement at the zoo. A big crowd was gathered around the lion's cage.

Simba was back. But he was not alone. Beside him sat a beautiful lioness with amber eyes and silken fur.

People were shouting. Children were laughing. Everyone was talking at once.

"Who is she?" they asked.

"Where did she come from?" they wanted to know.

"How did she get here?" they wondered.

Michael smiled up at his new friend, Buddy Brave. Only they knew the answer to the mystery at the zoo.

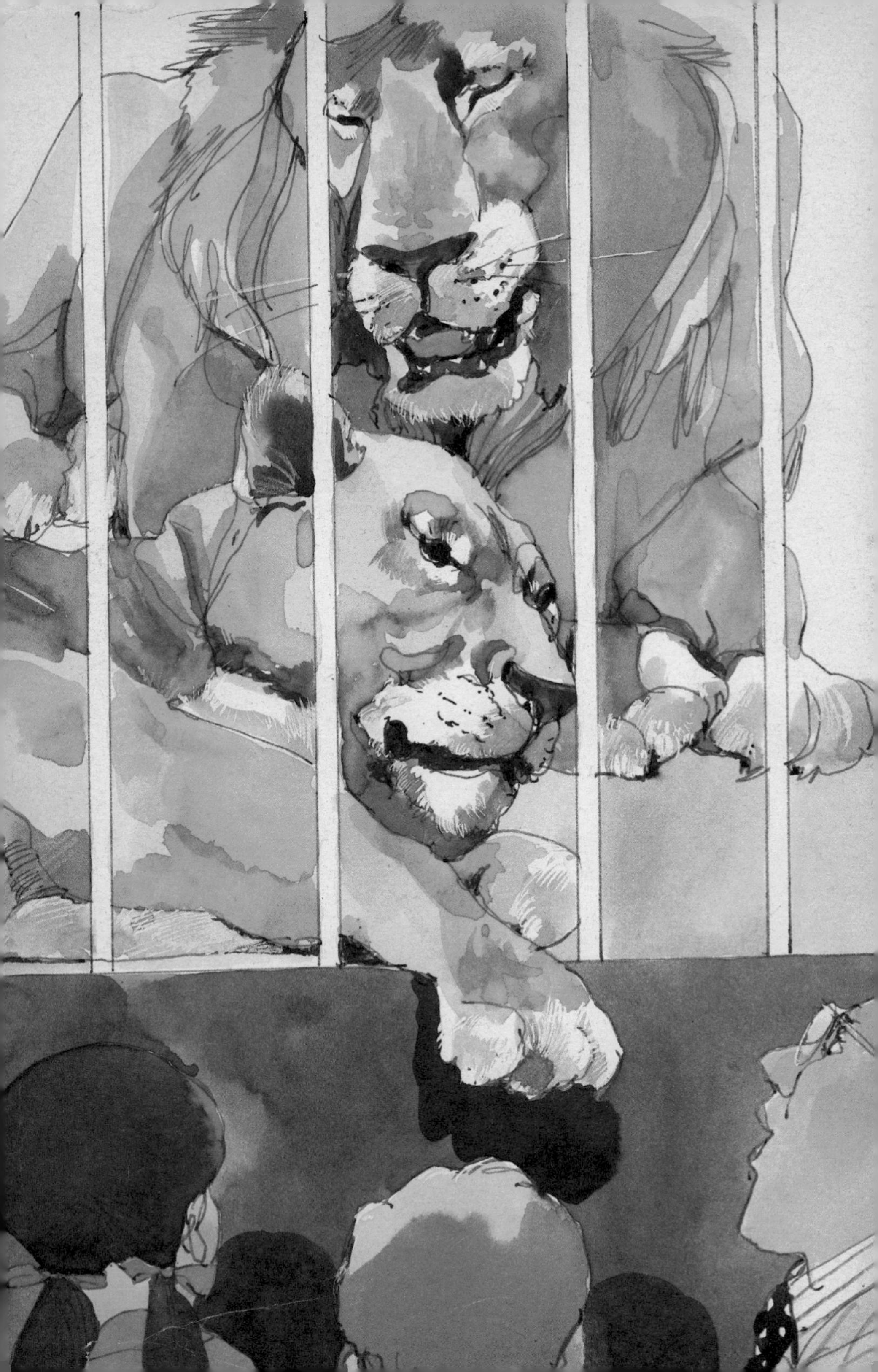

Now, every day when school is out,
Michael Andrew Kevin McCuller still
heads straight for the zoo.

He hurries past the zebras and the
giraffes and the monkeys.

He skips past the elephants and the
bears and the rhinoceros.

He waves to the balloon man and the woman who sells peanuts and popcorn.

He runs through the tunnel and over the bridge. He does not stop running until he reaches the lion's cage.

Then Michael Andrew Kevin McCuller puts down his books and says, "Good afternoon, Serena. Good afternoon, Simba. Tell me, how are you today?"

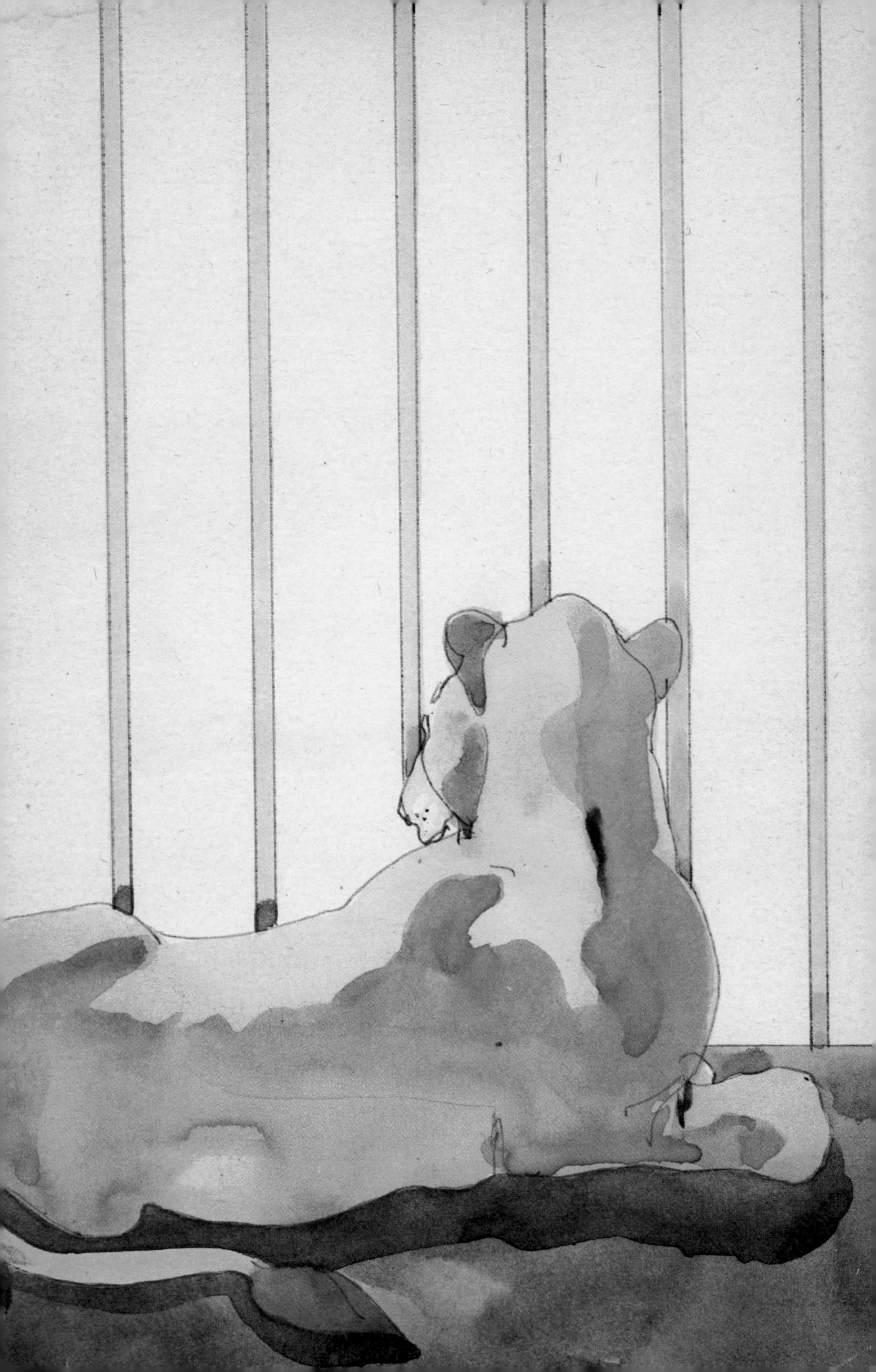

Serena purrs contentedly. And Simba
slowly rises to his feet, and tosses his tawny
mane, and blinks his golden eyes, and
answers:

"I am very happy, thank you, Michael.
Very, very happy."